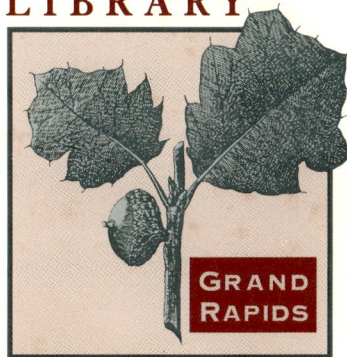

LIBRARY

GRAND
RAPIDS

FOUNDATION

A gift of the

Library Foundation

BUGATTI TYPE 35

There are two seats. One is for the driver. The other is for the "riding mechanic" who helped with repairs and looked out for road hazards.

Most Bugatti cars have a horseshoe-shaped **grille**.

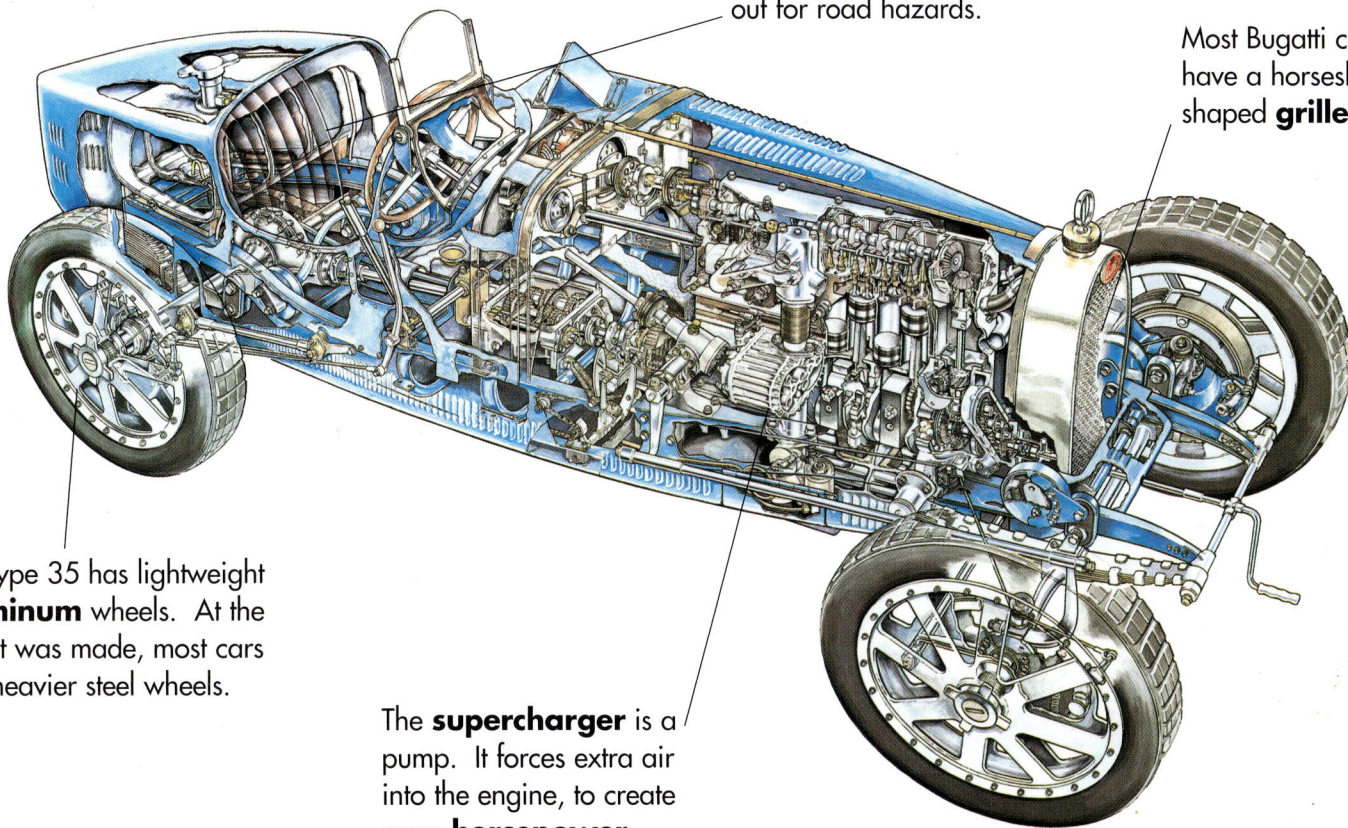

The Type 35 has lightweight **aluminum** wheels. At the time it was made, most cars had heavier steel wheels.

The **supercharger** is a pump. It forces extra air into the engine, to create more **horsepower**.

CONTENTS

Please visit our Web site at: www.garethstevens.com
For a free color catalog describing Gareth Stevens Publishing's
list of high-quality books and multimedia programs,
call 1-800-542-2595 (USA) or 1-800-387-3178 (Canada).
Gareth Stevens Publishing's fax: (414) 332-3567.

Library of Congress Cataloging-in-Publication Data

Gunn, Richard.
  Racing cars / Richard Gunn.
      p. cm. — (Cool wheels)
  Includes bibliographical references and index.
  ISBN-10: 0-8368-6829-3 – ISBN-13: 978-0-8368-6829-6 (lib. bdg.)
  1. Automobiles, Racing—Juvenile literature. I. Title. II. Series
TL236.G825   2006
629.228—dc22   2006042291

This North American edition first published in 2007 by
Gareth Stevens Publishing
A Member of the WRC Media Family of Companies
330 West Olive Street, Suite 100
Milwaukee, WI 53212 USA

© 2006 Amber Books Ltd.

Produced by Amber Books Ltd., Bradley's Close,
74–77 White Lion Street, London N1 9PF, U.K.

Project Editor: Michael Spilling
Design: SOL
Picture Research: Terry Forshaw and Kate Green

Gareth Stevens editorial direction: Valerie J. Weber
Gareth Stevens editor: Jim Mezzanotte
Gareth Stevens art direction: Tammy West
Gareth Stevens cover design: Charlie Dahl
Gareth Stevens production: Jessica Morris

Picture credits: Art-Tech/Aerospace: 5, 7; Getty Images: (Mike Hewitt) 9, (Sergio Lopez) 15, (Darrell Ingham) 17, (Robert Laberge) 19,
(Ker Robertson) 21, (Mark Thompson) 23; Giles Chapman Library: 11, 13; Corbis Images: (David Allio) 29.

Artwork credits: Art-Tech/Aerospace: 4, 6, 8; Mark Franklin (© Amber Books): 10, 12, 14, 28;
Alex Pang (© Amber Books): 16, 18, 20, 22, 24, 26.

Printed in the United States of America

1 2 3 4 5 6 7 8 9 10 09 08 07 06

COOL WHEELS

RACING CARS

by Richard Gunn

GARETH**STEVENS**
GS
PUBLISHING
A Member of the WRC Media Family of Companies

The Bugatti Type 35 is one of the most successful racing cars ever built. Compared to today's racing cars, it is not very fast. This car, however, won more than two thousand races.

It is a small car, so the driver does not have much room. It has a tiny windshield and no roof. There is little protection from the weather.

BUGATTI TYPE 35

First Year Made: 1924
Top Speed: 125 miles
(201 kilometers) per hour
0–60 miles (97 km)
per hour: 7 seconds
Power: 130 horsepower

Super Speed

The Type 35 was first made in 1924. Two years later, Bugatti made a different model — a supercharged version. It had a more powerful engine and was much faster.

The last Bugatti Type 35 was made in 1931. Only 340 were built. Today, these cars are very rare and expensive.

DID YOU KNOW?

The Italian carmaker Ettore Bugatti started the Bugatti car company. Before making cars, he studied to be an artist. Some people think his cars are like works of art!

JAGUAR D-TYPE

The D-type has a smooth shape that easily cuts through the air, allowing the car to reach high speeds.

The rear fin helps keep the car steady at high speed. The car's race number was painted on it, too.

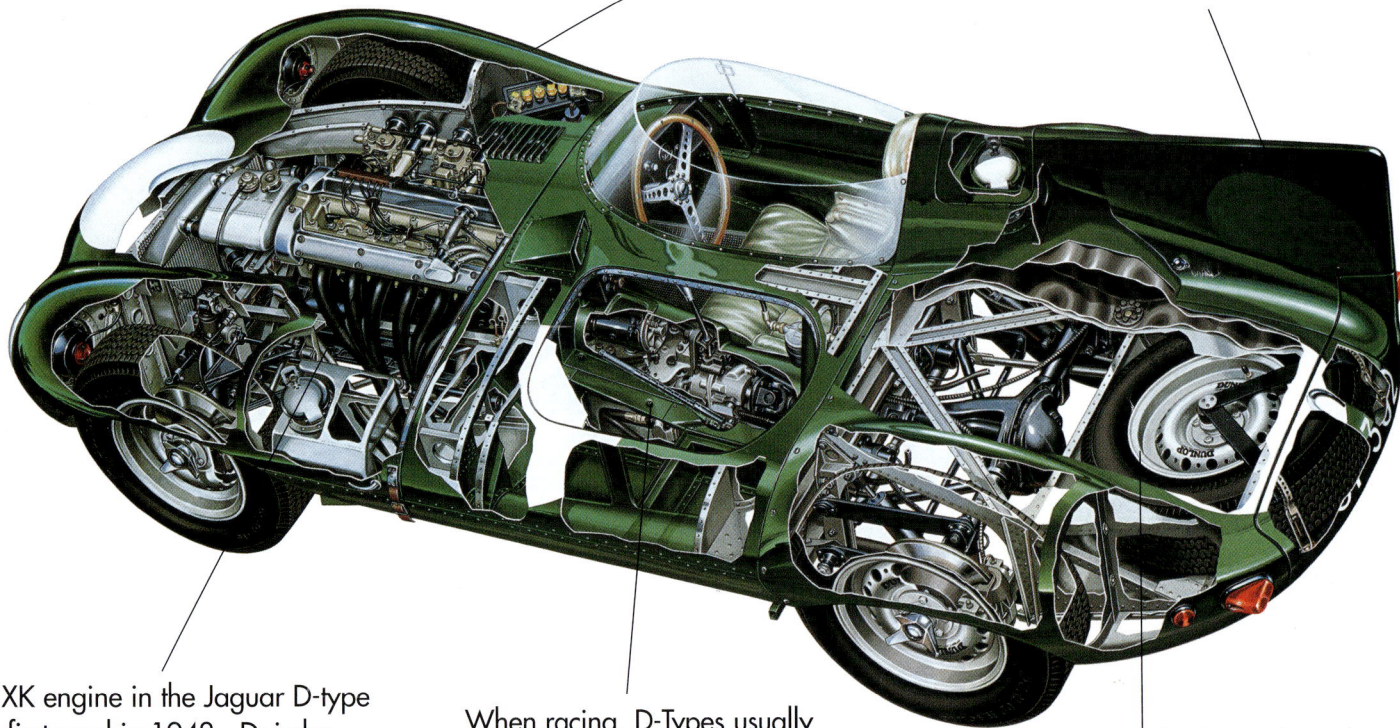

The XK engine in the Jaguar D-type was first used in 1948. Daimler limousines were still using the same engine in 1992.

When racing, D-Types usually had just a driver, but there was space for a passenger.

The D-type's trunk only has room for the spare tire.

The Twenty-Four Hours of Le Mans is one of the world's toughest races. For almost every year since 1923, it has taken place in Le Mans, France, each June. The cars drive day and night. Jaguar first won in 1951, using a car based on one of its passenger cars. Jaguar wanted to win again, so it built the D-type.

JAGUAR D-TYPE

First Year Made: 1954
Top Speed: 162 miles (261 km) per hour
0–60 miles (97 km) per hour: 4.7 seconds
Power: 250 horsepower

Winning Le Mans

The first of the D-types was made in 1954. The D-type had the same engine that Jaguar used in its passenger cars. Its body was **aerodynamic,** so it could cut through the air easily.

The D-type was very fast. It won many races, including Le Mans. It won the Le Mans race three years in a row.

DID YOU KNOW?

Jaguar also made a road version of the D-type, called the XKSS. Only sixteen were made before the factory that made them burned down, in 1957.

FERRARI 250 GTO

Air gets sucked in through the twelve intake pipes. The **carburetors** below the pipes mix this air with fuel.

The car's body is made of aluminum, which is much lighter than steel.

The **chassis** is made of thin steel tubes.

At high speeds, the engine can get very hot. Removable hatches at the front let extra air in for more cooling.

The Ferrari 250 GTO is a very special racing car. Between 1962 and 1964, only thirty-nine were built. Many people think the 250 GTO is the best car Ferrari ever made.

Power and Speed

Designers used a wind tunnel to test the body to see if it was as sleek as possible. It is made of

Left: The small grille in front was unusual at the time, but Ferrari wanted an aerodynamic shape for the car's body.

FERRARI 250 GTO

First Year Made: 1962
Top Speed: 170 miles (274 km) per hour
0–60 miles (97 km) per hour: 6.1 seconds
Power: 300 horsepower

lightweight aluminum. Beneath the body is a chassis made of thin steel tubes welded together. This **spaceframe** is light but strong.

The engine is a V12. It has twelve **cylinders** arranged in a V-shape. Every engine was tested before it was put in a car. The fast GTO rarely lost on racetracks.

DID YOU KNOW?

When new, the Ferrari 250 GTO cost $18,000. Since then, the price has skyrocketed. Today, a GTO can cost millions of dollars — if you can find one to buy!

FORD GT40

This car has a bubble-shaped roof so that tall drivers can sit comfortably inside!

The GT40 is a mid-engine car. Its engine is right behind the driver.

The "gullwing" doors are hinged at the top. They open up and out. When open, they look like a gull's wings.

"Knockoff" hubs fasten the wheels to the car. When a tire needed changing, they could be taken off quickly.

In 1963, Ford was going to buy Ferrari, but the deal fell through. People at Ford were angry. They set out to beat Ferrari on the racetrack. At the time, Ford did not build racing cars. It had to design a new car that was just for racing. This car was called the GT40. The GT40 soon started winning many races.

FORD GT40
First Year Made: 1964
Top Speed: 165 miles (266 km) per hour
0–60 miles (97 km) per hour: 5.5 seconds
Power: 500 horsepower

V8 Power

To make the GT40 reliable, Ford kept the design as simple as possible. The GT40 had the same kind of V8 engine that Ford used in its passenger cars.

The GT40 was very dependable. In long races such as Le Mans, it kept going when other cars broke down. The GT40 won at Le Mans in 1966, 1967, 1968, and 1969!

DID YOU KNOW?

The Ford GT40 got its name from the fact that it is just 40 inches (102 centimeters) tall. "GT" comes from the Italian words *Gran Turismo*, meaning "Grand Tourer." It is a name often used for fast cars that travel long distances.

SUBARU IMPREZA RALLY CAR

One seat is for the driver. The other seat is for the navigator, who reads a map and gives directions.

The engine is a flat-four. Its four cylinders are laid flat instead of upright.

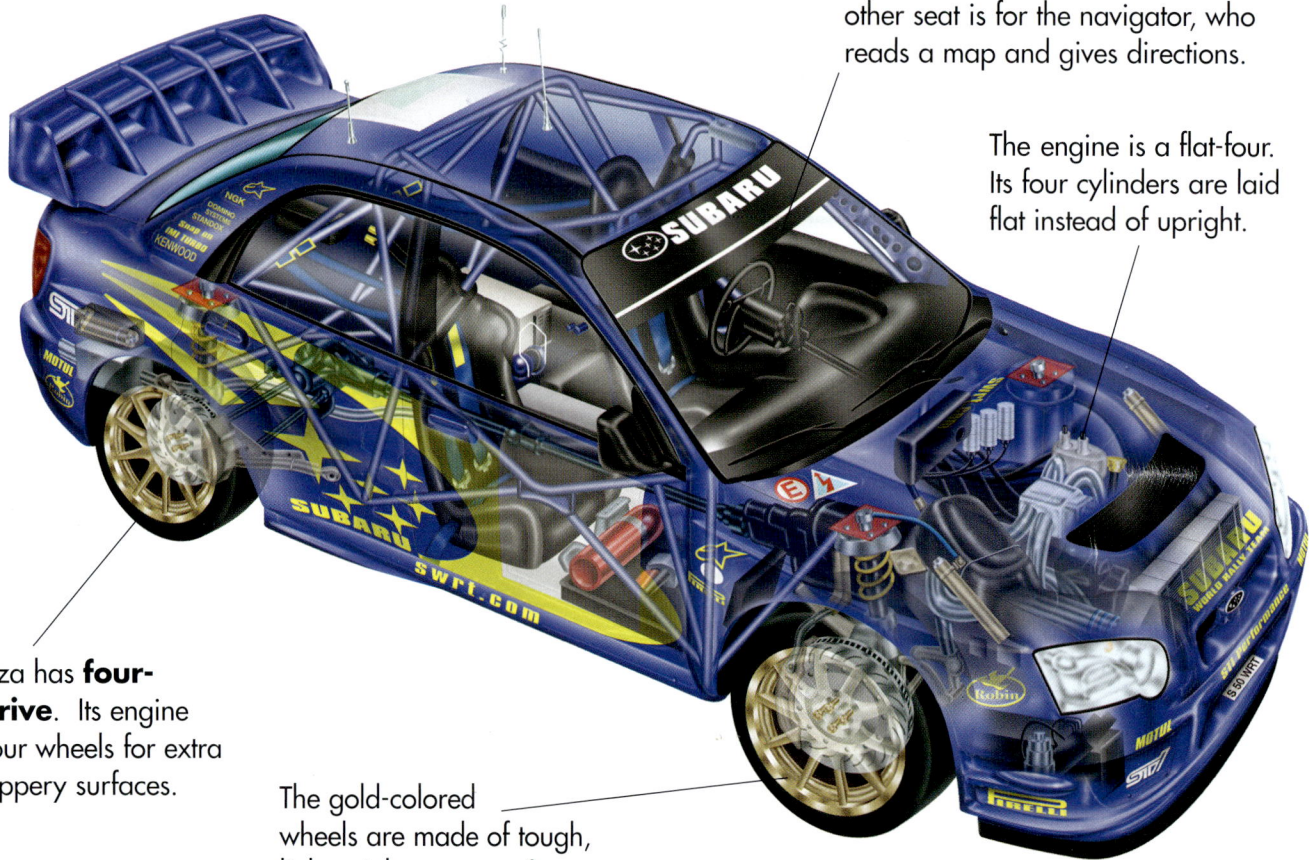

The Impreza has **four-wheel drive**. Its engine turns all four wheels for extra grip on slippery surfaces.

The gold-colored wheels are made of tough, lightweight **magnesium**.

Rallying is a kind of racing. Cars race on public roads and off-road trails. The Subaru Impreza has won many rallies since it first started racing in 1993. All the cars are painted in the blue and gold of Subaru's racing team.

A Different Model

The Subaru World Rally Championship (WRC)

SUBARU IMPREZA

First Year Made: 1993
Top Speed: 155 miles (250 km) per hour
0–60 miles (97 km) per hour: 4.3 seconds
Power: 300 horsepower

cars look very similar to Subaru's WRX passenger models. The rally team's cars, however, are very different. The rally cars have more powerful engines and stronger **suspension** to handle the tougher roads. They also have lightweight parts. Cutting down on weight helps the cars go faster. Subaru keeps changing its rally cars, making them better for each new racing season.

DID YOU KNOW?

The latest rally Imprezas have special monitors that let the driver or navigator select from eight different screens. These screens tell them if the car has problems.

13

FERRARI F1 CAR

The **cockpit** is specially made to fit a particular driver. The steering wheel has to be removed for a driver to climb in and out.

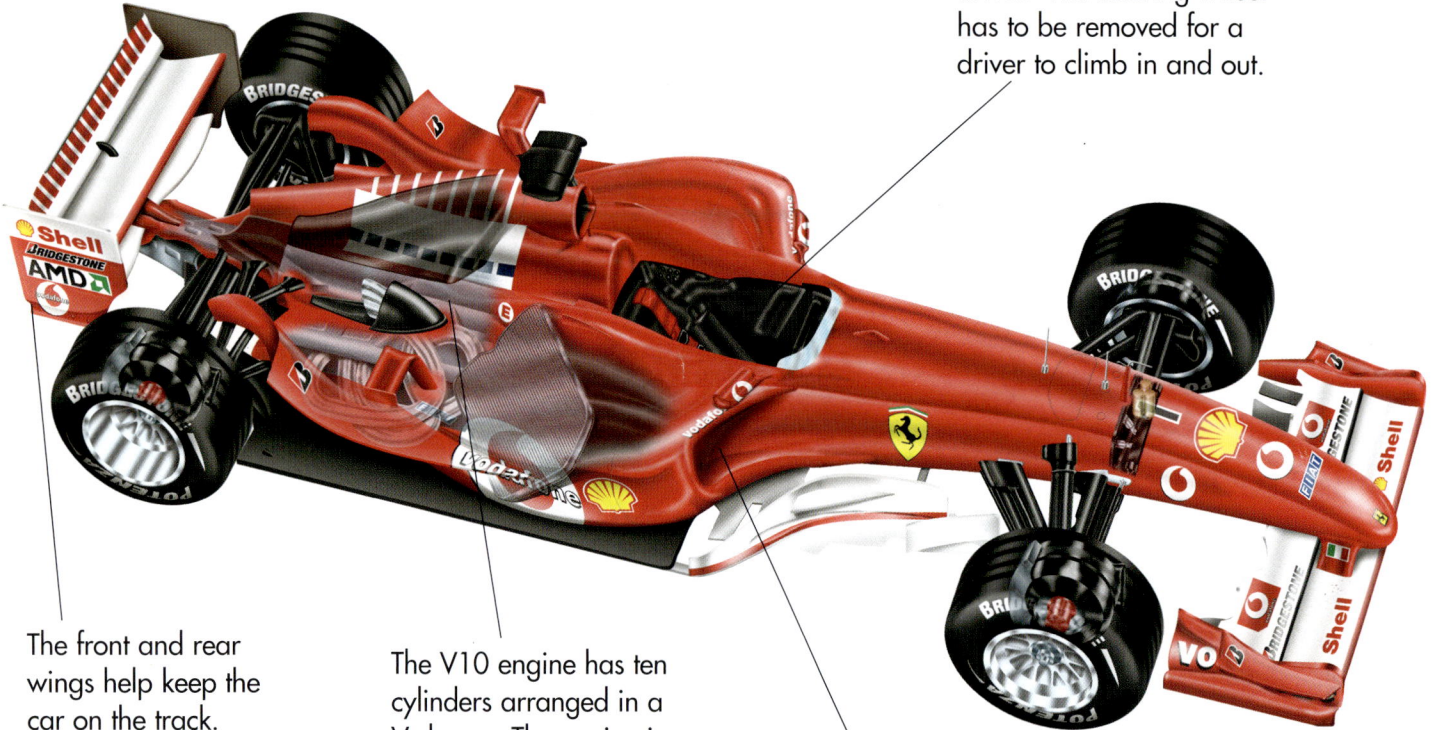

The front and rear wings help keep the car on the track. Air flowing past them pushes down on the car.

The V10 engine has ten cylinders arranged in a V shape. The engine is in the middle of the car, for better balance going around turns.

Big side scoops take in air for the two **radiators** that cool the engine.

Formula 1, or F1, is the most glamorous and expensive type of car racing in the world today. F1 has millions of fans worldwide.

Ferrari is one of the most successful car makers in F1 racing. The company also makes beautiful and expensive road cars that are popular throughout the world.

Left: The large air intake behind the driver takes air to the engine. The air mixes with the fuel.

FERRARI F1 CAR

First Year Made: 1998
Top Speed: 235 miles (378 km) per hour
0–60 miles (97 km) per hour: 2 seconds
Power: 900 horsepower

Schumacher's Success

Michael Schumacher is Ferrari's main driver. In the picture above, he is driving in Barcelona, Spain, in January 2005.

The Ferrari team builds new cars every year, but lately the improvements have been very small. Any changes have to follow the rules of the sport, which are very strict.

F1 cars are among the fastest and most advanced race cars in the world.

DID YOU KNOW?

Michael Schumacher has driven for the Ferrari team since 1996. Winning five World Championships from 2000 to 2004, he has made Ferrari the best-known F1 racing team.

INDY CAR

Tilting the rear wing changes how much the car is pushed down by air.

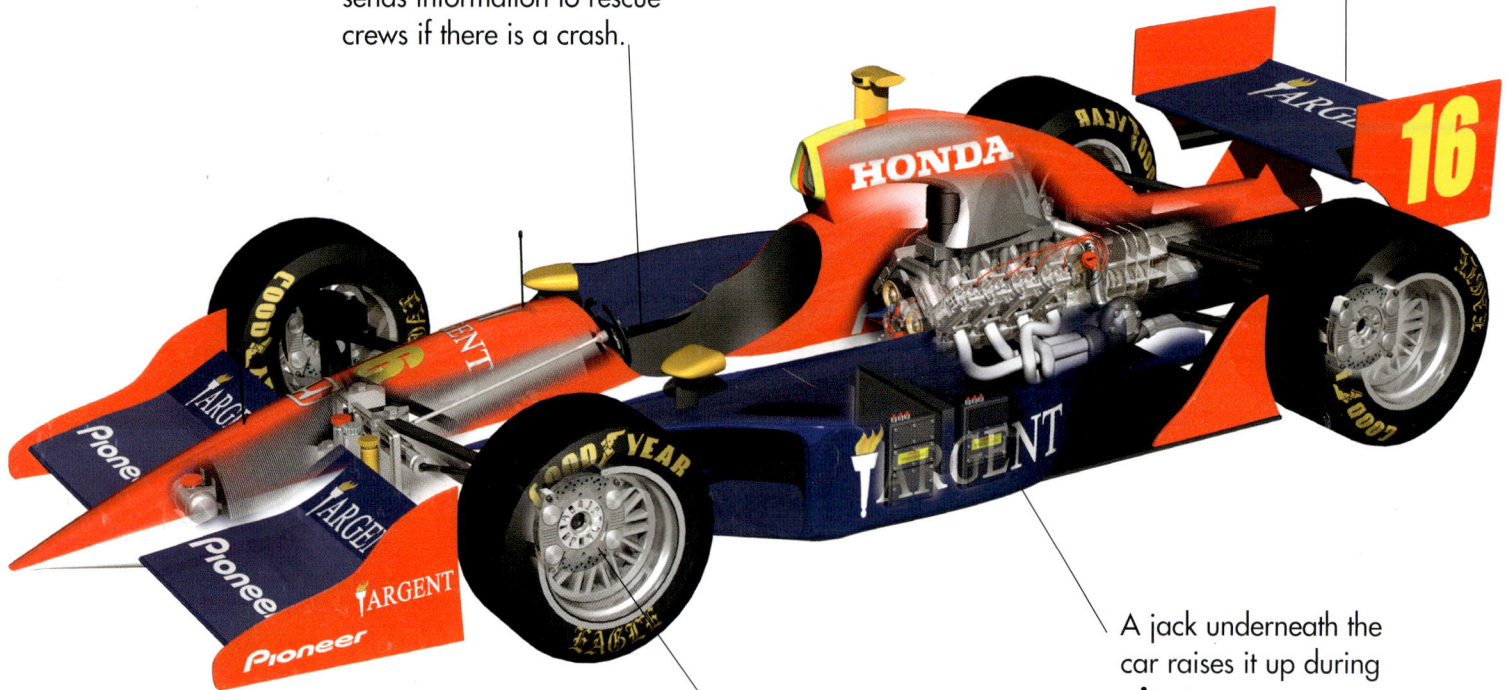

A device in all Indy cars sends information to rescue crews if there is a crash.

A jack underneath the car raises it up during **pit stops**.

Powerful brakes slow the car at high speeds.

In IndyCar racing, drivers race in open-cockpit, single-seat cars. These cars are similar to F1 cars. The races are only held in the United States. Most drivers are men, which is one reason Danica Patrick is so unsual.

Rookie of the Year

Danica Patrick drives for the Rahal Letterman team. She has only been

Left: During an IndyCar race, all four tires can be changed in seconds. The car can be raised off the ground by pushing a button that operates the jack underneath.

INDYCAR

First Year Made: 2006
Top Speed: 222 miles (357 km) per hour
0–60 miles (97 km) per hour: 2 seconds
Power: 650 horsepower

racing Indy cars since 2005, but she has done very well. She won the Rookie of the Year award at the end of her first season. She also became the first woman driver to lead the Indianapolis 500, one of the most difficult IndyCar races. On the track, she often reaches speeds of more than 200 miles (322 km) per hour.

DID YOU KNOW?

Indy cars get their name from the Indianapolis, or "Indy," 500 race. The 500-mile (805-km) race has been held every Memorial Day weekend since 1911.

CHAMP CAR

All current Champ cars use the same Ford Cosworth V8 engine, which has a **turbocharger**.

The rollbar protects the driver if the car crashes and rolls over.

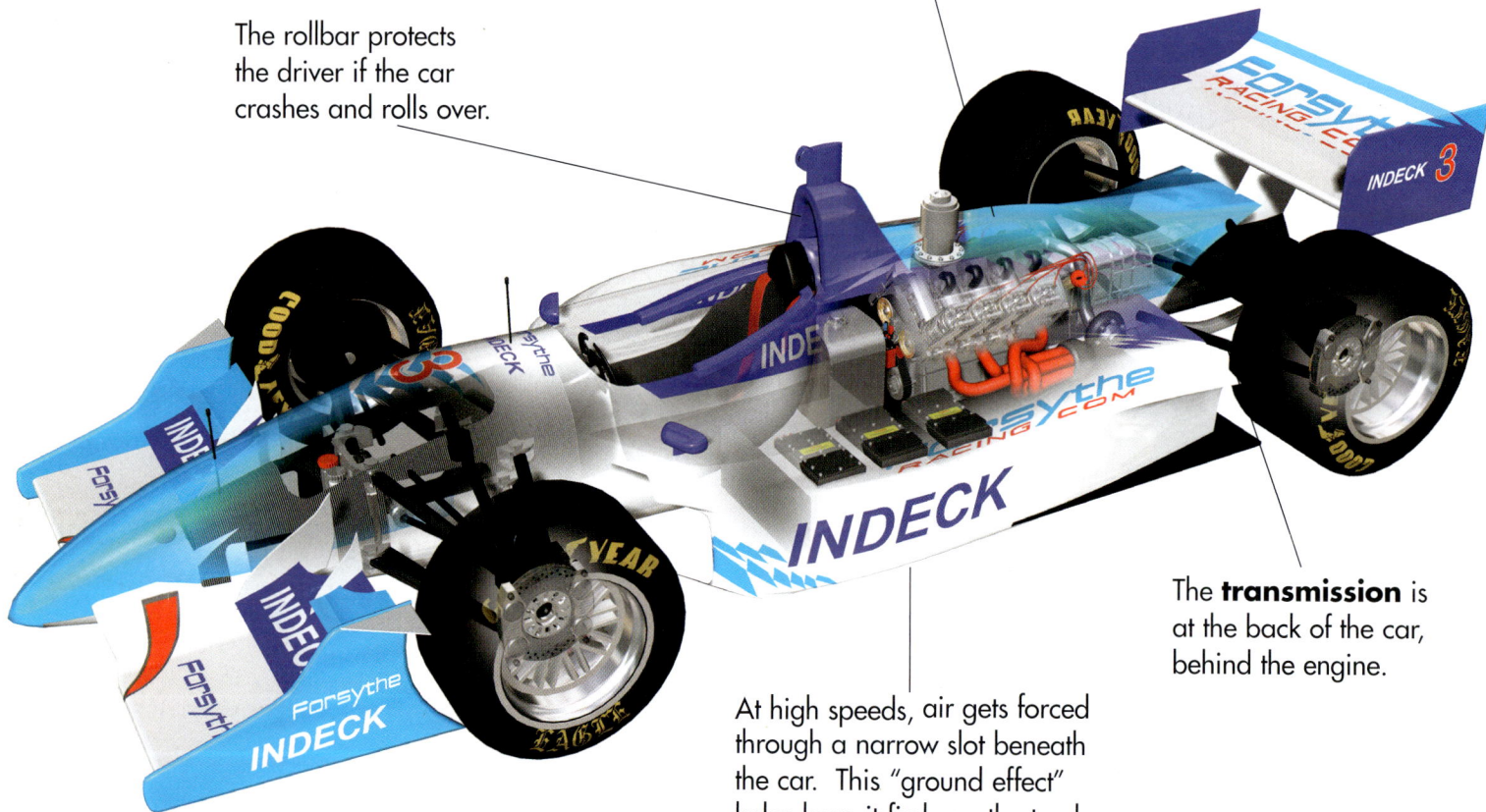

The **transmission** is at the back of the car, behind the engine.

At high speeds, air gets forced through a narrow slot beneath the car. This "ground effect" helps keep it fimly on the track.

Champ cars — short for "Championship cars" — look a lot like Formula 1 cars, but they use turbocharged engines that run on methanol. This special racing fuel creates a lot of power, so the cars can reach very high speeds. Running at such high speeds, Champ cars are very exciting to watch.

Left: Like most race cars, a Champ car has rear-wheel drive. Its engine turns the rear wheels. The rear tires are very wide, to give extra grip on the road.

CHAMP CAR

First Year Made: 2006
Top Speed: 240 miles (386 km) per hour
0–60 miles (97 km) per hour: 2.2 seconds
Power: 850 horsepower

Most Champ Car World Series races take place in the United States. The main races are in California and Oregon. Races are also held in Australia, Canada, and Mexico.

Paul Tracy

The Champ car pictured above has the blue and white colors of the Forsythe racing team. Paul Tracy drives for this team. He won the championship in 2003.

DID YOU KNOW?

The special **exhaust** pipes on Champ cars help keep down noise when the cars race on city streets.

CORVETTE C5-R

The rear wing on the C5-R helps keep the car on the ground when racing at high speed.

When racing in the dark, the Corvette uses a different nose section with extra lights that are very powerful.

Regular Corvettes have **fiberglass** bodies, but the C5-R body is made of **carbon fiber**.

The exhaust pipes are on each side of the car.

Left: Racing Corvettes are usually painted bright yellow. In 2003, however, the C5-Rs were painted red, white, and blue, after they beat Ferrari in the American Le Mans Series.

The Chevrolet Corvette has been around since 1953, and it has changed a lot through the years.

CORVETTE C5-R

First Year Made: 1999
Top Speed: 200 miles (322 km) per hour
0–60 miles (97 km) per hour: 0.5 seconds
Power: 620 horsepower

In 1999, a racing version came out called the C5-R. This Corvette had a carbon-fiber body instead of a fiberglass one, and it also had a wing on the back.

From U.S. to Europe

The C5-R used a large V8 engine. In 2000, the engine got even bigger. With the extra power, the C5-R won almost every race it entered. In 2002, for example, it won eight out of the ten races in its class. The car has also driven in the American Le Mans Series and European GT Championships.

The C5-R has now been replaced by the Corvette C6-R, which has many improvements.

DID YOU KNOW?

In 2004, the Corvette Racing team won every race that it entered with a C5-R. None of the cars even broke down!

AUDI R8 ENDURANCE RACER

The transmission is computer-controlled, so the **gears** can be changed quickly.

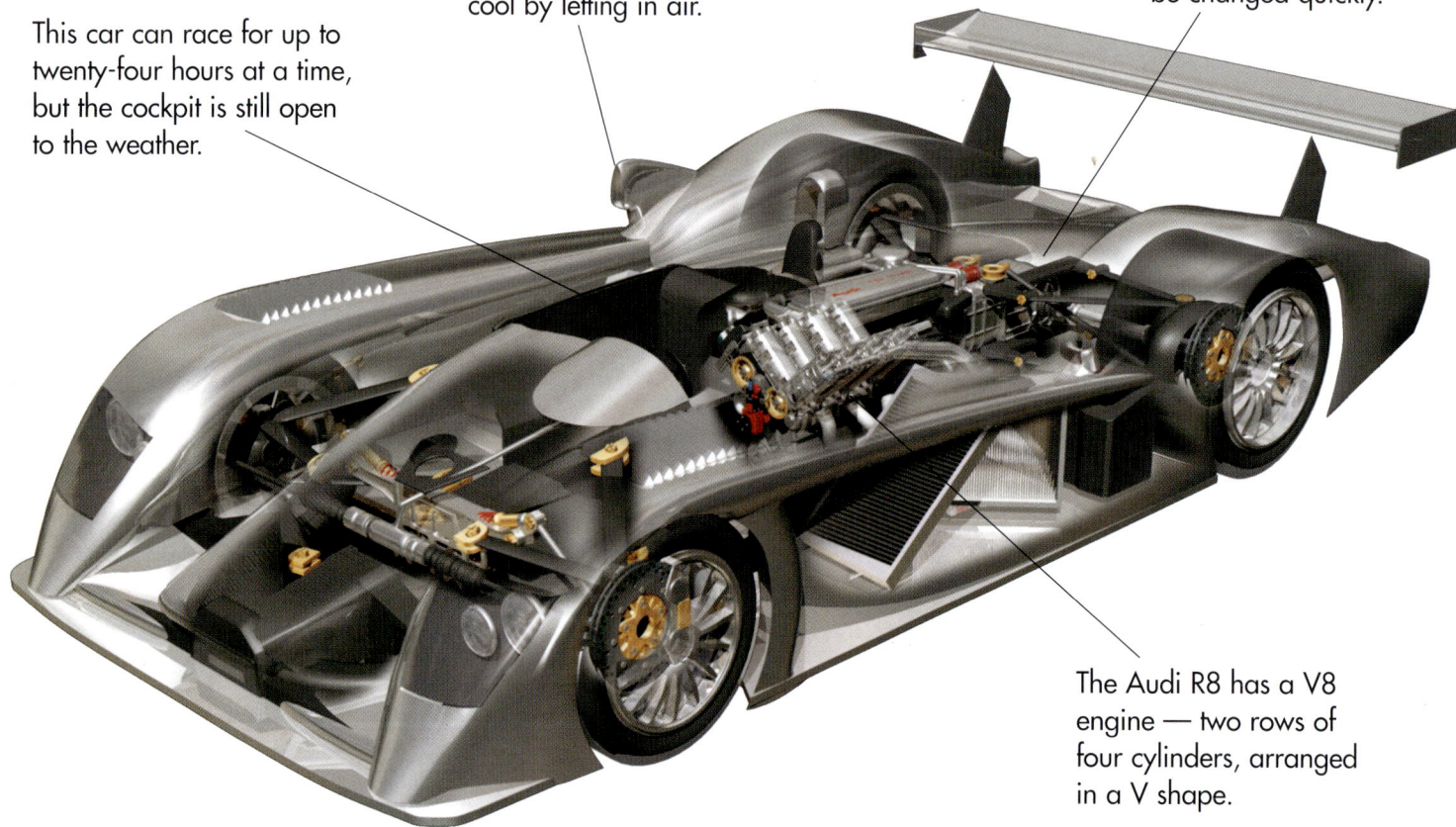

Air scoops help keep parts cool by letting in air.

This car can race for up to twenty-four hours at a time, but the cockpit is still open to the weather.

The Audi R8 has a V8 engine — two rows of four cylinders, arranged in a V shape.

Today, the Audi R8 is the most successful **endurance** racing car of the twenty-first century. It competes in long-distance races in both North America and Europe, and it has won many races since it first appeared in 2000.

Number One

Audi R8s have won the Twenty-Four Hours of

AUDI R8 IMSA

First Year Made: 2000
Top Speed: 205 miles (330 km) per hour
0–60 miles (97 km) per hour: 3.3 seconds
Power: 625 horsepower

Le Mans every year from 2000 to 2005, except 2003. That year, a Bentley using an R8 engine won! R8s have also won the American Le Mans Series five times in a row, from 2000 to 2004. The R8 is successful because it is a fast but safe car, and it does not often break down. Even when it does break, it is easy to fix, so it can rejoin a race quickly.

DID YOU KNOW?

The gearbox on an Audi R8 can be changed in less than five minutes during a race. On other cars, this job takes between one and three hours.

23

NASCAR RACING CAR

Roof flaps pop up if a car goes into a spin. They help keep the car from lifting off the ground and rolling over.

The V8 engine uses a carburetor instead of **fuel injection**, which is used on most modern racing cars.

NASCAR racing can be very dangerous. A **rollcage** protects the driver.

The suspension and brakes are adjusted for every race so they are the most effective for the track.

NASCAR races take place in the United States, mostly on oval tracks. The cars have bodies that look similar to passenger cars.

The rules for NASCAR do not allow cars to use modern **innovations**, such as fuel injection or automatic transmissions. The cars, however, are still fast and powerful.

Left: The famous "Number Eight" Chevy of Dale Earnhardt, Jr., races very close to the ground. Not much air can get beneath the skirting to slow down the car.

CHEVROLET MONTE CARLO

First Year Made: 2000
Top Speed: 217 miles (349 km) per hour
0–60 miles (97 km) per hour: 4 seconds
Power: 800 horsepower

Safety First

In NASCAR, all cars must meet strict safety rules. On fast tracks, tires must have an inner liner. It is like a second tire inside the main tire. The liner helps the driver keep control if there is a blowout.

Most of the cars have **skirting** added to the bottom edge of the body. It stops air from getting underneath and slowing down the car.

DID YOU KNOW?

NASCAR racing grew out of a time when bootleggers (makers of illegal alcohol) **modified** their cars to outrun the police. They eventually began holding races with their cars.

TOP FUEL DRAGSTER

Air passing over the wings pushes the car down onto the track.

Dragsters race in a straight line, so they do not need to turn. They can have very small wheels in front.

A parachute opens at the rear of the car to help slow it down after a race.

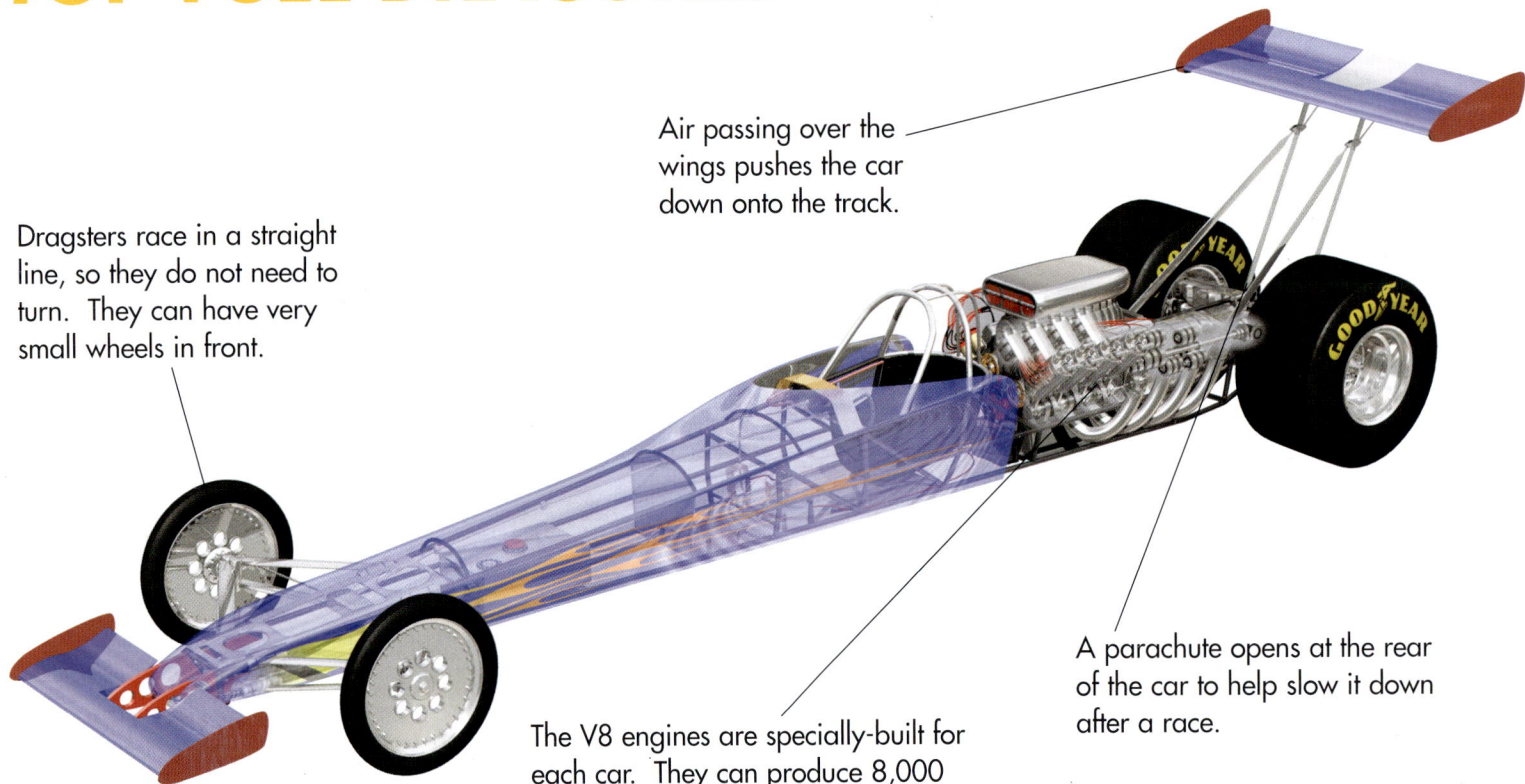

The V8 engines are specially-built for each car. They can produce 8,000 horsepower — more than eight times the power of other racing engines.

Top fuel dragsters **accelerate** faster than any other cars in the world. Traveling in a straight line at very high speeds, drivers try to cross the finish line in the shortest time.

Dragters use a special fuel called nitromethane. This fuel is so powerful that it can also be used to power rockets.

TOP FUEL DRAGSTER

First Year Made: 2006
Top Speed: 336 miles (540 km) per hour
0–60 miles (97 km) per hour: 0.6 seconds
Power: 8,000 horsepower

Short and Quick

Dragsters race a short distance — only about a quarter of a mile (400 meters). A race is over in seconds. When it ends, parachutes open at the back of the cars. They help slow down the dragsters and keep them from crashing. In one race, a dragster may use 12 gallons (45 liters) of fuel — almost as much as a whole tank of fuel in some passenger cars!

DID YOU KNOW?

The engines in top fuel dragsters are so loud that people nearby have to wear earplugs to stop the noise from hurting their ears!

FUNNY CAR

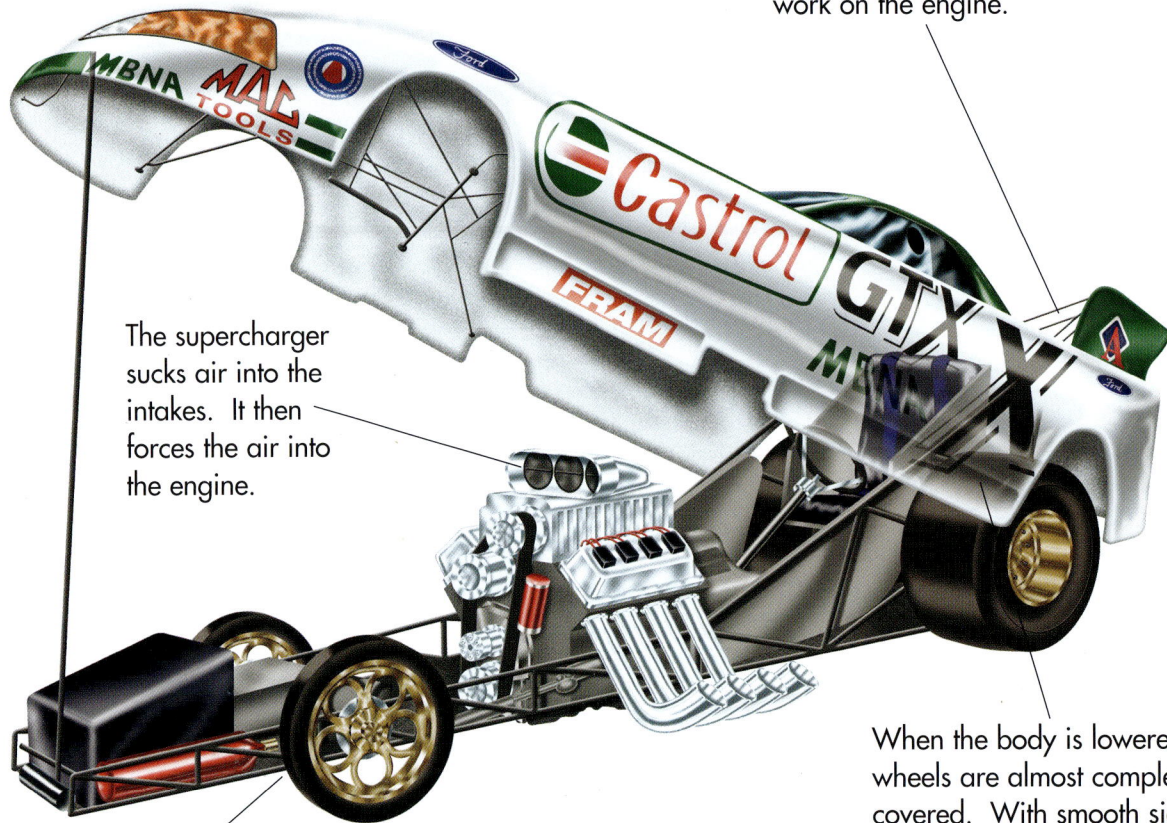

The body has hinges at the back. Mechanics can flip up the whole body to work on the engine.

The supercharger sucks air into the intakes. It then forces the air into the engine.

When the body is lowered, the wheels are almost completely covered. With smooth sides, the car can cut through the air.

The bottom of the car is only 3 inches (8 centimeters) from the ground.

Funny cars are similar to top fuel dragsters, but they are shorter and their engines are in front. They also have full bodies, made of lightweight carbon fiber.

The bodies look like racing versions of well-known passenger cars. John Force's funny car, which is pictured here, has a body that looks like a Ford Mustang.

FUNNY CAR — JOHN FORCE

First Year Made: 2006
Top Speed: 333 miles (536 km) per hour
0–60 miles (97 km) per hour: 0.5 seconds
Power: 7,000 horsepower

Five-second Funny

Like top fuel dragsters, funny cars have huge rear wheels. A lot of rubber touches the track, so the tires have a good grip for quick starts.

These cars are so fast that a race usually lasts only about 5 seconds. Sometimes, the cars do not finish the race. They may break down, crash, or catch on fire!

DID YOU KNOW?

John Force holds the current speed record for funny cars. He reached 333.6 miles (537 km) per hour, traveling a quarter of a mile (400 m) in 4.7 seconds,

GLOSSARY

aluminum — a lightweight metal.

accelerate — increase in speed.

aerodynamic — having a shape that slips easily through the air.

carbon fiber — a material using threads of carbon that is much stronger and lighter than steel.

carburetors — devices that mix fuel and air for an engine.

chassis — the frame of a car, which supports the engine, transmission, suspension, and body.

cockpit — the space in a racing car where the driver sits.

cylinders — spaces inside an engine where fuel and air explode to create power.

endurance — the ability to do something for a long time.

exhaust — the gases an engine creates when it burns fuel and air.

fiberglass — a lightweight material that is made with glass threads and plastic.

four-wheel drive — a system that sends an engine's power to all four wheels.

fuel injection — a system that sprays fuel into an engine; most engines now use fuel injection instead of carburetors.

gears — small, toothed wheels. A car's transmission has many gears, which change the speed of the car.

grille — the opening in a car that lets in air to cool the radiator.

horsepower — the amount of power an engine produces, based on how much work one horse can do.

innovations — improvements or better ways of doing things.

magnesium — a very strong, lightweight metal.

modified — made changes to something.

NASCAR — National Association for Stock Car Auto Racing.

pit stops — short stops during a race for refueling, changing tires, or carrying out repairs.

radiators — devices that cool the liquid flowing through an engine, to keep the engine from getting too hot.

rollcage — a strong metal cage inside a racing car that protects the driver during a crash.

skirting — panels around the bottom of a car's body that stop air from flowing underneath, so the car goes faster.

spaceframe — a strong, light chassis frame that is made up of many small steel tubes joined together.

supercharger — a pump that forces extra air into the engine to improve power.

suspension — the parts that attach the wheels to a car and help the car ride smoothly on bumpy surfaces.

transmission — the part of a car that takes power from the engine and sends it to the wheels.

turbocharger — a pump that gets driven by the force of exhaust leaving an engine; it pumps extra air into the engine, for more power.

FOR MORE INFORMATION

Books

Cars. Speed! (series). Jenifer Corr Morse
(Blackbirch Press)

Fast Cars. Wild About (series). David Kimber
(Ticktock Publishing)

Formula One Cars. Wild Rides (series).
A. R. Schaefer and Betty Carlan (Edge Books)

Nascar. DK Eyewitness Books (series). James Buckley
(DK Children)

Racing Cars. Look Inside Machines (series). Jon Richards
(Stargazer Books)

Superfast Cars. Ultimate Speed (series). Mark Dubowski
(Bearport Publishing)

Web Sites

Fact Monster: Professional Auto Racing
www.factmonster.com/ipka/A0771589.html

Inner Auto Parts: Explore the Marvel of the Automobile
www.innerauto.com

Motorsport Mathematics
www.racemath.info

World Almanac For Kids: Auto Racing
*www.worldalmanacforkids.com/explore/sports/
autoracing.html*

INDEX